APR 0 8 20

P9-DTA-558

**READ MORE BOOKS
BY SUZANNE SELFORS!**

Wedgie & Gizmo

Wedgie & Gizmo vs. the Toof

SUZANNE SELFORS

WEDGIE & GIZMO

VS. THE GREAT OUTDOORS

Illustrated by

Barbara Fisinger

KATHERINE TEGEN BOOKS
An Imprint of HarperCollinsPublishers

Katherine Tegen Books is an imprint of HarperCollins Publishers.

Wedgie & Gizmo vs. the Great Outdoors
Copyright © 2018 by HarperCollins Publishers
All rights reserved. Printed in the United States of America.
No part of this book may be used or reproduced in any manner
whatsoever without written permission except in the case of brief
quotations embodied in critical articles and reviews. For information
address HarperCollins Children's Books, a division of HarperCollins
Publishers, 195 Broadway, New York, NY 10007.
www.harpercollinschildrens.com
Library of Congress Control Number: 2018933384
ISBN 978-0-06-244775-3
Typography by Carla Weise
21 22   CG/LSCH   10 9 8 7 6

First Edition

For Kyle and Bean,
a girl and her dog.

FAMILY

Mom

Jasmine

Jackson

Wedgie

ALBUM

Abuela

Dad

Gizmo

Elliot

CHAPTER 1

GIZMO

GREETINGS TO YOU, DEAR READER.

It is I, Gizmo the Evil Genius, once again giving you a front-row seat to my exciting and Evil Life. Today I have excellent news to share. Whilst nibbling on a post-breakfast snack of celery leaves, I overheard the humans discussing their plans to take a vacation. They are leaving today and will be gone for an entire week. Do you know what that means?

Party time!

What a perfect opportunity to host the event of the century. I shall invite all my fans and followers. It will be a magnificent affair.

I still have access to the Elderly One's credit card, so no expense will be spared! I will hire a party decorator. There will be streamers, a fountain of sparkling water, and an ice sculpture of me wearing my crown. But no balloons. Their dreadful explosions startle me and make me piddle. We cannot have the future King of the World piddling at his own party!

I shall also order the very best food—juicy fruits, sweet seeds, and vegetable peelings. Of course, there will be a tub of mini marshmallows, which the humans do not allow me to eat because they "are not good for me."

Hear this, humans—I shall be the one who chooses what does and what does not go into my belly. No one tells Gizmo the Evil Genius what to eat!

There will be speeches about me, given by me. And songs about me, sung by me. And when the party is over, I shall hand out signed photos of my handsome, furry face. My guests will be so pleased.

Oh, I do hope the humans leave soon so I can begin to—

What is happening? The ground is shifting! My entire Eco Habitat is being lifted into the air. I rush to my sleeping chamber's window. Elliot, my loyal servant, is carrying me out of our bedroom and down the hallway. Where are we going?

ELLIOT: It's okay, Gizmo. Don't worry. You'll like it there. You might even make some new friends.

It is not unusual for one of the humans to interrupt me during an important moment, such as nap taking or Evil Plan making. When the girl child, Jasmine, picks me up, it is usually for a session of squeezing and kissing. When the Elderly One picks me up, it is usually for an afternoon of television watching. And Elliot often carries me into the food-preparation room for snacks. But

rarely does anyone pick up my entire house!
I fear something is amiss.

MOM: Is everyone ready to go?

DAD: I hope you all remembered to pack
bathing suits, pajamas, extra
shoes, extra socks, extra underwear,
toothbrushes, sunglasses, and a
jacket because it gets cold at night.

JASMINE: Dad, you already told us what to pack at least a million times.

DAD: Just making sure.

JACKSON: I packed ALL my underwear!

MOM: Oh dear, it looks like Jackson *only* packed underwear. Don't worry, it'll just take me a minute to fix this.

Elliot carries me outside. The sun is shining; the birds are tweeting. It is a perfectly lovely day for party planning. But why is Elliot setting my Eco Habitat onto the back seat of the minivan? I stand on my hind legs to peer through my window, but my view is blocked by the seat in front of me. Why am I back here? I do not have time for a field trip. I have a party to plan.

I demand answers! Let me out of this automobile or you shall all feel my wrath!

CHAPTER 2

WEDGIE

JASMINE'S CALLING MY NAME. I *LOVE* JAS-mine! I run down the hallway, my cape flapping behind me. My cape is very important. When I wear it, I'm Super Wedgie and I have Super Powers, like running real fast. I slide on my tummy because the floor's slippery. Here I come. Sliding on my tummy. Uh-oh, it's a corner. I can't slow down.

Wham!

I'm okay. It's just a wall. Jasmine calls my name again. Here I come. I'm almost there.

But wait. Sometimes it's good when Jasmine calls my name. It means I'm getting a treat or we're going to the beach. But sometimes it's bad when she calls my name. It means she's trying to trick me into doing something I don't want to do.

Like take a bath.

Or go to that terrible place where the lady in the white coat lives.

I crawl under the couch. Stay away from me. I don't want a bath! And I really don't want to see the lady in the white coat. I scoot back as far as I can until my rump hits the wall. Jasmine's arms reach for me but she can't find me. I'm using my superpowers of hiding. No one can find Super Wedgie when he's hiding.

JASMINE: Don't worry, Wedgie, you're not getting a bath and you're not going to the vet. Mom, he won't come out from under the couch.

MOM: You'll have to tempt him with a treat.

You can't find me, Jasmine, because I'm Super Wedgie. Yep, that's me, and I will protect my pack. There are six people in my pack. There's Mom and Dad and Jasmine and Jackson and Elliot and Abuela. There's also Furry Potato. I LOVE my pack!

My job is to keep my pack safe. So that means I'm very busy. I'm always on the lookout for danger, like other dogs who want to steal our sticks and poop in our yard. Or squirrels who want to live in our trees and throw nuts on our heads. Squirrels are bad. I don't love squirrels. But sometimes Super Wedgie needs to hide and that's what I'm doing.

Oh, what's that? I sniff the air. It smells sweet. It smells cinnamony. My heart starts beating real fast. A shiver darts up my back. It smells like . . .

. . . cookie!

I dart forward. Give me that cookie! Please oh please oh please can I have that cookie? Cookie, cookie, cookie—

JASMINE: Got him!

MOM: Great. Put him in the car.

JASMINE: Wedgie, stop whining. There's no reason to be scared.

Jasmine picks me up. Now she's carrying me. Where are we going? Why doesn't she give me the cookie? There's Dad. He opens the car door. Jasmine puts me inside the car. Then she gives me the cookie. I eat it in one bite. I LOVE that cookie!

I look at Jasmine. Why am I in the car? Where are we going? She sits next to me and pulls me onto her lap. Dad and Mom get into the car. Elliot and Jackson get into the car. Wait! I smell something cheesy. I turn around. I stand on Jasmine's lap and look over her shoulder.

Hey! I see Furry Potato. Hello, Furry Potato. He's sitting next to Abuela. And she's eating cheesy snacks. I LOVE cheesy snacks. I stare at her, real hard. And whine. Please oh please oh please give me a cheesy snack. She does! I eat it. It tastes so good! Can I have another one?

MOM: Abuela, please don't feed those to Wedgie. They're not healthy for dogs.

ABUELA: I've seen that dog eat goose poop. Do you think *that's* healthy?

MOM: Well, no, of course not.

ABUELA: At least a cheesy puff has cheese.

Abuela gives me another snack. Yum!

My whole pack's in the car. We're going somewhere. What a great day. I'm so happy. I LOVE my pack!

I lick Jasmine's face. I'm a happy dog.

CHAPTER 3

GIZMO

AS THE AUTOMOBILE DRIVES DOWN THE ROAD, I check my appointment calendar. As I suspected, there is no field trip listed for today. I grunt with dissatisfaction. I am a hostage, being driven somewhere against my will. How many times must I remind these humans to discuss all travel plans with me?

How very rude of them!

I should be home, getting ready for my grand party. Instead I am stuck here, with that drooling canine staring at me from the other seat. What is his problem? Does he not have a comic book to read or a sudoku puzzle to entertain him during the ride?

I accept a cheesy puff from the Elderly One. As I chew, I think about the ways I might seek revenge on the humans for cavy-napping me. I make a mental list.

LIST OF WAYS TO GET MY REVENGE
1. Order a box of crickets and let them loose in the house.
2. Steal all the toilet paper and hide it behind Maytag Dryer.
3. Leave my droppings in the Raisin Bran cereal.

The automobile stops moving. The engine shuts off and the humans open the doors. I am curious. What sort of field trip is this? Maybe I will see some of my stuffed ancestors at the Natural History Museum—ancient saber-toothed rodents who once roamed the continent.

Or perhaps the city has finally erected a statue dedicated to me. I have written numerous letters to city hall requesting the statue. I even sent them a design to save them time. I am so very considerate.

Elliot lifts my Eco Habitat. He carries me from the car. He walks past a store that sells coffee and past another that sells books. Then we stop.

I lean out my habitat's window to get a better view.

BOB'S PET STORE AND PET HOTEL

If you are one of my new readers, you may not know that I was born in a pet store. *Swampy's Pet Shop* to be precise. I do not remember my parents, for they went to live with a human child, as did my three littermates. I was the last of my family to leave the store. Why? The answer is obvious. Because I am *not* a pet. I am special and everyone knows that.

So I bided my time, not waiting for an owner, but waiting for someone who would serve me. And that someone was Elliot. Occasionally he makes a mistake, like selecting an unripe strawberry or forgetting to tell me about a field trip, but mostly he is a true and loyal servant.

But I am still confused as to why we are here. I do hope the humans are not buying another canine. Can you imagine having two canines in one house? The noise! The destruction! I would need to visit a spa three times a week just to settle my nerves.

As Elliot carries me inside, I detect the dry odor of reptile and the spicy scent of gerbil. There is a saltiness to the air, coming from the large tanks where colorful fish swim. But then another scent hits my nose and my little heart nearly stops.

A feline. Or, as you call it, a cat.

This is not the time to panic. Cats are rodent hunters, and I am a member of the rodent family. I am also plump and would most likely taste delicious, thanks to my diet of cheesy puffs and breakfast cereal.

"Beware, cat!" I squeak. "Do not mess with me!"

To my dismay, I do not smell other cavies in this store. Notice that I do not use the term *guinea pig*. Never will I call myself by that name. We are cavies, proud rodents who have nothing to do with pigs. But alas, it appears I am alone.

BOB: Hello, how may I help you folks?

DAD: We're the Washington family. We called about boarding our pets while we're on vacation.

BOB: Fill out these forms, please. Is there anything we should know about your pets? Do they have any special needs?

JASMINE: Wedgie likes to wear his cape. It's his favorite thing.

ELLIOT: Gizmo's just a regular guinea pig. He doesn't need anything special.

Regular guinea pig? How could my loyal servant say such an insulting thing? There is nothing regular about me. I come from a long line of purebred Peruvian cavies. I can read and write. And never forget that my brain is the size of three peas. Not two. Three!

BOB: You can bring your pets back here into our boarding area. We've got one other critter staying in our pet hotel tonight.

How very interesting. I have never stayed in a pet hotel. Elliot carries me into another room and places my Eco Habitat onto a shelf.

BOB: Have fun, folks. I'll call if there's any trouble.

ELLIOT: See you in a week, Gizmo. Be good.

A week? But what about my grand party? I shake my fists through the window. There had better be a spa at this hotel. And room service!

The humans walk away. No one has offered me a heated towel or a fluffy bathrobe. This must be one of those cheap one-star hotels. Oh, how I suffer!

I take a look at my surroundings. To my right sits a stack of cans. To my left sits a small cage. I sniff. The occupant of the cage is definitely from the rodent family, but I am not familiar with its scent. The cage is full of wood chips, upon which sits a toilet paper tube.

"Hello," I call. "I am Gizmo the Evil Genius and future King of the World. What and who might you be?"

There is no reply.

"Do you know if this hotel has bed turndown service?" Still no reply. How rude.

Then I spy golden fur inside the toilet paper tube. The creature is asleep. How

shocking. I use my toilet paper tube for sharpening my teeth. I would never sleep in such a place!

I yawn, then curl into a ball. It is time for my prelunch nap. Once I am refreshed, I shall check out the room-service menu.

CHAPTER 4

WEDGIE

I *LOVE* THIS PLACE! IT SMELLS LIKE THE BEST place ever. What's this? It's a box of chew toys. And what's this? It's a basket of squeaky toys. Oh, look over here, I found a mouse. Hello, mouse! And there's another mouse. Hello, other mouse! And there's a snake. Hello, snake! And here's a lizard. Hello, lizard! I wag my rump. What's this? I stand on my hind legs. It's a bunch of frogs. Hello, you guys!

Hey, what's that sound? Something's growling. I get on my belly. I peer under the shelves. What's under here? Hey! It's a cat! A Cat! A Cat! A Cat!

DAD: Wedgie, stop barking.

There's a Cat! A Cat! A Cat!

JASMINE: Wedgie, you're scaring that poor
kitty. She's the pet-store cat and
that means she lives here. Be nice.

Jasmine's pulling me away. But I wanna chase that cat. I wanna chase that cat so bad I'm shaking all over. Please let me chase that cat. Oh please oh please oh please.

Now Jasmine's pulling me into a room. Hey, why are we in this room? The cat's out there. Jasmine gets on her knees and looks into my eyes. She kisses my nose.

JASMINE: I'll see you in one week. I'll miss you.
Be good.
MOM: Yes, please be a good dog, Wedgie.
JASMINE: He will. Won't you, Wedgie? You'll
be a good dog, right?
JACKSON: Bye-bye, Gizmo. Bye-bye, Wedgie.

Jasmine kisses my nose again. I LOVE Jasmine! I lick her face. Can we go chase the cat now? I do not love cats. Cats need to be chased. Squirrels need to be chased too. But right now I wanna chase that cat.

Jasmine's walking away. I start to follow but someone shuts the door. Hey, I'm still in here. You left me in here. Hello? Hello? I'm in this room. Where are you? Come get me. Let me out!

I hear a squeak. Oh look, there's Furry Potato. He's in this room with me. What's he doing up on that shelf? Hello, Furry Potato. Don't worry, because I'm Super Wedgie, so I'm gonna use my superpowers to get us out of this room.

I turn in circles in front of the door, my cape flying. After I turn in circles, the door will open because I'm using my superpowers. Circle, circle, circle. Circle, circle, circle.

Huh?

I sit and stare at the door. How come my superpowers aren't working? I'm Super Wedgie and I need to be with my family. I need to protect them.

And I need to chase that cat.

Let me out!

CHAPTER 5

GIZMO

ONCE AGAIN, THE CANINE IS INTERRUPTING my nap with his barking. He knows how puffy I look when I do not get enough beauty sleep. He also knows that during my naps, I recharge my Evil Genius Brain. How can I look handsome and be super smart if I can't sleep?

Everything he does is aimed at destroying me. His life revolves around me. He should be grateful that I exist, for I have given him a purpose. Without me he would be just another drooling, useless beast.

However, I do need my sleep. I would dial the front desk of this hotel and complain, but they have not provided me with a phone. So I must put an end to this noise myself.

I climb out my Eco Habitat window and lower myself onto the shelf. I glance at my neighbor, who is still sleeping in the toilet paper tube. Barking does not seem to disturb that yellow creature. My ears, however, are sensitive to all sorts of noises.

Sounds I enjoy: the tearing of cardboard as a cereal box is opened, the pleasant drone of the narrator on the nightly news, and the rumble of the mail delivery truck as it brings me a package.

Noises I despise: the canine's whimpering, the canine's snoring, and the hiss of his dog farts. Basically, everything he does drives me nuts!

I walk to the edge of the shelf and peer down. There he is, staring at the door, barking. Does he not understand how to open a door? You must turn the knob, you fool!

I narrow my eyes as I spy his red cape. I discovered, many long weeks ago, that this corgi dog had somehow gotten his paws on the superhero cape that once belonged to the great Thor himself. And thus, he has turned himself into . . . Thorgi! My archnemesis!

Oh, how can I make him stop? Genius Brain, do not fail me! Then I remember the items that are stacked upon the shelf.

FISHY TAILS AND SQUISHY SNAILS STEW FOR CATS

Eureka! I shall hurl these cans downward where they shall make contact with Thorgi's head. That will teach him a lesson for disturbing my slumber. I slide a can to the edge, then give it a firm push. A thudding sound follows. I peer over. Drat! The can missed its target by a few inches. Thorgi turns, sniffs the can, then faces the door again and resumes his barking. I shall continue my assault. I push another can, then another, and another.

"Take that!" I declare. "And that!"

Thud.

Thud.

Thud.

I peer over. How can this be? Every can has missed its mark, but one can has opened upon impact, spilling its salty contents. Thorgi stops barking and begins to lap up the lumpy feast. While I welcome the silence, I know it will not last. As soon as the food is gone, he will start barking again.

There are more cans, larger than the others. Surely they will not miss their target.

PUMPKIN PULP FOR PUPPIES

With all my Evil Strength I push one of the larger cans. It teeters on the edge, then falls. Then I push the others. Push, push, push. Take that, and that, and that!

Thud.

Thud.

Thud.

I lean over the edge. Thorgi is lapping up orange goo from another can that has opened. I am perplexed. Flummoxed. My aim is usually perfect. How is it possible that every can missed its mark?

And that is when my gaze lands, once again, upon the red cape, and my Evil Genius Brain solves the mystery.

It was not my aim that was at fault. Of course not. Thorgi is in one piece, dear reader, because the cape has powers of protection. Why did I not see this before? If I can get my paws on Thorgi's cape, then he will be too weak to stop me and I can finally be rid of him. A new Evil Plan must be hatched immediately.

Muh-ha-ha!

Thorgi finishes eating and turns to face the door. He starts barking again.

What's this? The door opens and the hotel owner enters.

BOB: Oh no, look at this mess! You two are outta here!

CHAPTER **6**

WEDGIE

I DID IT! I USED **MY SUPERPOWERS OF BARK**-ing to get us out of that room. Whenever my pack forgets about me, I bark. And bark and bark. And my powers make them come back. And now we're in the car. We're going for a ride.

I LOVE going for a ride! Jasmine's here. I'm standing on her lap. Elliot's here. Now I'm standing on his lap. Jackson's here too. His lap is little but I stand on it anyway.

Hello, Family! Where are we going?

MOM: That was so embarrassing. I can't believe it. He said that in all his years of boarding pets, he'd never had a dog bark that much. And he'd never had a guinea pig destroy property.

JASMINE: Wedgie didn't like being locked in that room, Mom. Can you blame him?

ELLIOT: I guess Gizmo didn't like it, either.

ABUELA: The cavy is an evil genius.

DAD: Well, there's no time to find another place to board your pets, so it looks like we'll have to take them with us.

JACKSON: Yay!

JASMINE: Did you hear that, Wedgie? We're all going on vacation. Together!

Jasmine hugs me. I lick her face. Then I walk across everyone's lap. Back and forth, back and forth. I stand on my hind legs and peer over the seat. Abuela's in the back seat. I LOVE Abuela! She smells minty because she rubs minty cream on her knees. Minty

cream tastes minty. I don't love it.

Hey, Furry Potato's back there, in his special box. Hello, Furry Potato. We're going for a ride. Furry Potato squeaks at me. He sure is a nice potato.

What a great day this is! And I, Super Wedgie, will make sure to keep my whole family safe, for that is what I do—

Day or night,
Night or day,
I keep my pack safe,
Come what may.

JACKSON: Are we there yet?

MOM: We have a four-hour drive to get to the lake.

JACKSON: Yay! A lake! I'm gonna play in a lake!

ELLIOT: Four hours? Ugh. Can we watch a movie?

DAD: Mom and I decided that this would be a zero-technology trip. So no phones, no computers, and no iPads.

ELLIOT: What?

JASMINE: That's crazy!

ELLIOT: Not even in the car?

MOM: You'll have to entertain yourselves the old-fashioned way. It'll be good for you.

DAD: Yes, like we did when we were kids. We didn't have any of those gadgets and we had plenty of fun. We climbed trees.

MOM: We played hide-and-seek.

ABUELA: We went cliff diving, and raced cars, and parachuted out of airplanes. I miss those days.

ELLIOT: Can I parachute—

DAD and MOM: No!

I'm walking back and forth, back and forth. This window, then that window, then this window. There are cars on this side. There are trees on that side. I'm on Jasmine's lap, Jackson's lap, Elliot's lap, Jackson's lap, Jasmine's lap—

Jasmine uses her angry voice and says the word *stop*.

That is one of the words I know. It means that I am being a Bad Dog. I look into Jasmine's eyes. What do you want me to do? Do you want me to cuddle? I turn in a circle so I can get comfortable. But Jasmine pushes me off her lap.

JASMINE: Wedgie, move over.

ELLIOT: I'm soooooo bored.

MOM: Here, try this crossword puzzle.

JACKSON: Can I do it?

ELLIOT: No, Jackson, you're too little.

JACKSON: I don't like being little.

ELLIOT: Quit tugging on it. You can't even read yet!

JACKSON: Can, too!

JASMINE: Stop kicking me, Jackson.

I stand on Jackson's lap. Jackson, do you want to cuddle? Jackson smells like peanut-butter toast. His fingers are sticky. His cheek is sticky too. I lick his cheek. It tastes peanut-buttery. I stretch across Jackson's lap. He scratches behind my ear. I LOVE Jackson!

I close my eyes. I'm gonna go to sleep now.

JACKSON: Are we there yet?

CHAPTER **7**

GIZMO

THE ENGINE HAS STOPPED. CAR DOORS ARE opening and closing, which means we have reached our destination. This is good news, for I have much work to do.

In case you have forgotten, I recently realized that Thorgi's cape was protecting him, and I decided that I must take it. Without his cape, Thorgi will be a weak, ordinary canine. He will not be able to stop my quest to become King of the World!

I wish to get started. So I exit my Eco Habitat, hop onto some luggage, and look outside the car window.

I am most pleased to report that we did not return to the horrid pet hotel. What a disappointing place. As soon as I get home, I shall write the following review:

"The service at Bob's Pet Store and Pet Hotel was the worst. I would rather sleep in a toilet paper tube."
Zero stars from Gizmo the Evil Genius

It appears that we are parked in some sort of primeval forest. How odd. The humans are outside. What are they talking about? I step on a button and the car window lowers. I prick my ears to hear their voices.

JACKSON: Can I climb that tree? Can I go see that lake? What's that over there? Can I go over there?

MOM: Jackson, calm down. We're here for a whole week. You'll have lots of time to play.

DAD: The first thing we need to do is set up the tents.

JACKSON: Hey, can I do that? Wait for me!

Tents? I narrow my eyes. What have these humans planned? I rise up on my tip-toes to get a better view, and that is when I see the sign:

WELCOME TO
CHIPMUNK LAKE
CAMPGROUND

Campground? Hold on an Evil Minute. Gizmo, the future King of the World, does not camp! What is that noise? I hear a squeak. There it is again. I turn and look at my Eco Habitat. My toilet paper tube is moving. What trick is this? A nose pokes out the end of the tube. Then a furry, golden face appears.

A stowaway!

I am in shock, I tell you. Utter shock! My shelf neighbor was so unhappy at Bob's Pet Hotel that it hitched a ride in my Eco Habitat.

I scurry down the luggage. Then I rise to my full height and point a finger. "This is the private domain of Gizmo the Evil Genius, and you are trespassing," I inform it. "Who are you?"

There is no response. Does this creature not speak my language? How rude! All I can see are two black eyes and tufts of yellow fur. Gerbil faces are not that furry. Rat faces are longer, with piercing red eyes. I shall force it out of the toilet paper tube so I can get a good view.

I walk to the other side of the tube, then I stretch my back leg until I make contact with the creature's rump. I push with all my Evil Might. But it will not budge. I do not have time for this nonsense. I must perfect my Evil Plan to separate Thorgi from his cape!

And then an idea develops in my Evil Genius Brain. What rodent can resist food? I scurry to my secret stash of seeds—aka my SSS.

Please be advised that I cannot reveal the location of my SSS, dear reader, for I do not want word to spread. Secret stashes are of the utmost importance. You never know when a volcano might erupt or a sinkhole might appear, making it difficult for a servant to get to the grocery store.

I am about to set a sunflower seed in front of the toilet paper tube when the car doors open. The humans have returned. I must warn them.

> **MOM:** This forest is really lovely.
>
> **ABUELA:** It is full of bugs. I don't like bugs.
>
> **DAD:** Okay, everyone, carry as much as you can. It'll take a few trips to get all our stuff down to our campsite.
>
> **JACKSON:** Can I carry Gizmo?

ELLIOT: No, you might drop him.

MOM: Jackson, Gizmo's cage is too big for you.

JACKSON: Aw. How come I never get to do anything?

I stand on my hind legs and put my little paws around my mouth and holler, "We have a stowaway!" I point to the toilet paper tube. "Remove it immediately. I have no desire to share my home. Send it hence!"

JASMINE: Why is Gizmo squeaking like that?
ELLIOT: I don't know. Come on, Gizmo. Our campsite is cool. It's right next to the lake.

My Eco Habitat is lifted and taken out of the car. Why are the humans not listening to me?

Once again, I shall have to take matters into my own paws. I will use my Evil Brain and rid myself of this pest, once and for all!

Right after I take my presupper nap.

CHAPTER 8

WEDGIE

WHAT ARE THOSE THINGS? THEY LOOK LIKE tiny squirrels. Hey, people, do you see all the tiny squirrels?

I do not love tiny squirrels. Tiny squirrels need to be chased. I'm gonna chase them. I'm gonna chase all of them. I'm gonna chase them until they go away because that's what Super Wedgie does. He chases all the tiny squirrels until they go away.

Super Wedgie to the rescue!

CHAPTER **9**

Gizmo

AFTER WAKING FROM MY NAP, AND AFTER eating a supper of alfalfa pellets, sunflower seeds, and dried cranberry, I look out my Eco Habitat window. I find myself in some sort of green dome.

> **JASMINE:** Mom, why do we have to share a tent with Jackson?
>
> **ELLIOT:** We can't tell scary stories if he's here.

JASMINE: And I won't be able to sleep 'cause he'll kick me all night.

JACKSON: I'm gonna sleep in the middle!

JASMINE: Why can't he sleep with Abuela in her tent?

MOM: Because we promised Abuela that if she came on this trip, she could have a tent to herself.

ELLIOT: That's not fair.

DAD: How about this—when you're eighty years old, you can have a tent all to yourself. For now, you two need to stop complaining and start enjoying this wonderful vacation. And stop being mean to your little brother!

It would appear that I am to spend this human vacation trapped inside a tent with children. I am the future King of the World. My tent should be private *and* shaped like a castle!

A sound startles me. The toilet paper

tube is moving. The stowaway is still here?

Suddenly, a golden rump pops out of the tube, followed by a very round, very fluffy golden body. I notice a tiny collar with the tag: *Butterball*. Whoever named the little creature did an excellent job, for not only is it the color of butter, but it is as round as a ball.

Dear reader, brace yourself, for what I am about to describe is disgusting, at best. The creature waddled up to my feeding trough and stuffed the entire contents—seeds, nuts, and grains—into its cheeks, until each cheek was as large as its body.

I gasp. What sort of power is this?

Then I understand. I am looking at a hamster—one of the most popular pets at Swampy's Pet Shop because human children seem to adore them. I have always found hamsters to be lazy creatures who sleep twenty-three hours a day. I am a fan of sleeping, but one should not sleep for more than twenty-one and one-half hours daily.

The hamster looks at me and blinks. "Aha!" I cry, pointing a paw. She scurries back to the toilet paper tube. Then she takes a deep breath and manages to squeeze her giant, swollen head back into that tube, without so much as a thank-you for the food.

A stowaway *and* a thief. Ordinarily I would admire such Evil Behavior, but not when I am the victim. Something must be done. A new Evil Plan must be made. Fortunately, I keep a stack of papers in my office for such important matters.

CAMPER: How long are you folks staying?
DAD: We're driving home on Sunday.
CAMPER: Be sure to take that hike up to Chipmunk Waterfall. It's a beauty.
MOM: Thanks. We will.

I glance at my calendar. If I am to stay in the primeval forest until Sunday, then I might as well make the best of it. Why not meet the locals and spread the word while I'm here? I imagine that I will meet raccoons, badgers, possums, field mice, rabbits, wolverines, foxes, wolves, and chipmunks, of course. I will tell them about my uprising and they will join my Evil Horde. Brilliant!

Thus, I will delay my important Gizmo party, and instead focus on taking over the world, one campground at a time.

Best add that to my list . . .

MY NEW EVIL PLAN by GIZMO THE EVIL GENIUS

1. Get rid of the stowaway and thief known as Butterball!

2. Separate Thorgi from his cape so that he is powerless!

3. Recruit all the forest critters into my Evil Horde and take over the campground. Without his superpowers of protection, Thorgi will be unable to stop me!

What a glorious plan! I am about to tape the plan to my Eco Habitat's wall when the tent shakes. Thorgi rushes in and sticks his nose right through my window and begins sniffing my backside. How rude! I retreat to the corner, where he cannot reach me.

Then I wait for the perfect moment to strike. . . .

CHAPTER 10

WEDGIE

I LOVE THIS TENT. IT SMELLS LIKE THE FURRY Potato in here. Hello, Furry Potato. I LOVE the way you smell. Do you have any poop that I can eat? Your squeaks sound so funny. Your fur tickles my nose. Did you see all the tiny squirrels? Tiny squirrels are bad!

Hey, what's this? It's a new smell. What's that new smell? It's coming from the toilet paper tube. I LOVE toilet paper tubes. They're fun to chew but they aren't fun to eat. Why does this toilet paper tube smell different? Is there something inside? Hey, people! There's something inside the toilet paper tube!

JASMINE: Wedgie, stop barking.

ELLIOT: Ugh, it's so crowded in here.

JACKSON: Will someone read me a story?

Furry Potato squeaks again. Does he want to play with me? I wag my rump. Come on, Furry Potato. Let's play. I stick my head in as far as it will go.

Ouch! Furry Potato just bonked me on the nose. Why would Furry Potato bonk me on the nose? I LOVE Furry Potato. I look at him. I whine. I feel sad. Now he's biting my cape. Why's he biting my cape? I LOVE my cape! Now he's pulling on my cape. He's pulling real hard. My head is stuck. I can't move. Furry Potato is pulling on my cape. Now he's got my cape!

Hey! That's my cape!

He's squeaking. He's jumping up and down. Give me back my cape, Furry Potato! People! Furry Potato has my cape!

ELLIOT: Wedgie, get your nose out of Gizmo's cage. He doesn't like that.

JASMINE: Wedgie, stop barking!

JACKSON: Will someone read me a story? Please?

JASMINE: Can't you just look at the pictures? I want to read my own book.

JACKSON: You guys NEVER read to me anymore!

ELLIOT: Mom! Dad! Wedgie's trying to eat Gizmo!

DAD: Come on, Wedgie, you'd better sleep with us.

Dad's picking me up. Wait! I want my cape! My cape, my cape, my cape!

JACKSON: Here's your cape, Wedgie.

I LOVE Jackson! I lick his face. Jackson looks sad. Why does Jackson look sad? Don't worry, Jackson. Super Wedgie will keep you safe tonight. I won't let the tiny squirrels get you!

Dad ties the cape around my neck. I'm Super Wedgie again! Dad carries me out of the tent. Good-bye, Jackson! Good-bye, Elliot! Good-bye, Jasmine! Good-bye, Furry Potato! Good-bye, new smell inside the toilet paper tube!

CHAPTER 11

GIZMO

WHAT IS THAT RUCKUS? I POKE MY FURRY face out of my sleeping chamber. The sun has barely risen and yet it sounds as if thousands of birds are holding some sort of meeting. The chirping. The tweeting. Do they not know that their future king is trying to sleep?

But of course! They are celebrating my arrival. How considerate of them. Later today, I will take a stroll around the grounds, waving toward the treetops so the birds can gaze upon my magnificence. They may be birdbrains, but I shall find a place for them in my Evil Horde.

Then I scowl as I remember the events of last night. Victory was so close I could almost taste it. I had my Evil Paws on Thorgi's cape. It was mine. But the smallest human child reached into my habitat and took the cape. Then he returned it to the canine. That child must be a fan of superheroes. I detest super-heroes, especially the kind who drool and dig holes.

Thorgi may think that he has stopped me, but he will be surprised when I command my new army of forest minions to tackle him and take his cape!

Muh-ha-ha!

DAD: Kids, get up. It's time for breakfast!

JASMINE: I smell pancakes.

ELLIOT: And sausage.

JACKSON: Hey, wait for me. Wait for me.

"Good riddance," I say as the human children run from the tent. "Leave me in peace so I can begin my Evil Day." And what a gloriously Evil Day it will be!

I draw a star next to the most important item on my Evil Plan. Only an Evil Genius could come up with such an Evil, Evil Plan!

MY NEW EVIL PLAN by GIZMO THE EVIL GENIUS

1. Get rid of the stowaway and thief known as Butterball!

2. Separate Thorgi from his cape so that he is powerless!

★ 3. Recruit all the forest critters into my Evil Horde and take over the campground. Without his superpowers of protection, Thorgi will be unable to stop me!

In order to achieve my goals, I must first deal with item #1: Get rid of the stowaway and thief known as Butterball. I cannot leave her alone in my Eco Habitat, for she will surely find my SSS and stuff every seed into her cheeks. That would be a disaster, for out here in this primeval forest there is no way for me to replenish my supply.

Every rodent knows the importance of stashing food. Even canines know this, which is why Thorgi buries bones in the backyard. But he also buries socks and tennis balls. Why? Because his brain does not work properly. Even though the canine brain is bigger than three peas, it is a fact that 99.99 percent of the canine brain is dedicated to piddling, rump sniffing, and barking.

But 99.99 percent of the rodent brain is used for important things, and we rodents know that nothing is more important than filling our stomachs. So we do not stash stupid things, like socks and tennis balls. We keep secret stashes of seeds, which this golden invader will not have!

I knock on the toilet paper tube to get her attention. "Ball of Butter," I say, "the time has come for you to leave. I understand your desire to stay with me, your future king, for I am entertaining and awesome. However, I do not have the food supply to support the two of us. Therefore you must venture forth and find your own way."

She does not come out of the tube. I shall remove her myself! I open the front door to my Eco Habitat. Then I begin to roll the tube. The tube will not fit through the door,

so I turn it sideways and push it out, onto the tent's floor. Using my Evil Strength, I roll the tube across the sleeping bags and out the tent's opening. Once we are outside, I stop to catch my breath and to gaze upon my surroundings.

What I see nearly takes my breath away!

CHAPTER 12

WEDGIE

IT'S MORNING. I *LOVE* MORNING! I CRAWL out of my sleeping bag. I lick Dad's face. I walk across Mom's tummy. I grab one of Mom's socks. I stand outside Mom and Dad's tent. This is our new house. And this is our new yard. It smells nice out here. I can smell trees and dirt and wind. I piddle on this tree, then that tree. Then that tree over there. I dig a hole and bury the sock. It's my sock now!

This tree smells like tiny squirrels. I look up. I see lots of little eyes looking back down at me. Uh-oh. The tiny squirrels are here. Hey! I holler at them. You can't live in this tree. This is our yard. We live here! Stay away from my sock!

MOM: Wedgie, stop barking. You'll wake the other campers.

Mom puts a bowl in front of me. It's full of kibble! I eat my kibble. I piddle again. But I don't piddle on the tent. If you piddle on the tent they call you Bad Dog. I walk around the tents. I'll protect my new home and my new yard with my superpowers. I'll chase the tiny squirrels. I won't let them steal our sticks or our socks.

You hear that, tiny squirrels? If you try to steal anything, I'll chase you. Hey, what's going on over there? I smell pancakes. I LOVE pancakes!

MOM: What's the matter, Jackson?

JACKSON: I can't zip my pants.

MOM: Elliot, Jasmine, why didn't you help your brother?

JASMINE: Aw, Mom, he needs help with *everything*.

JACKSON: No, I don't!

Everyone's eating. Can I eat? I sit next to Jackson and wait for him to drop his pancake. Please oh please oh please drop that pancake. It looks so yummy. I want it real

bad. I whimper. I wiggle. I stare. Super Wedgie needs that pancake.

Jackson drops it! Right into the dirt. I gobble it up. It tastes sweet and crunchy. I lick Jackson's fingers. Thank you, Jackson, for that yummy pancake.

Now I sit next to Elliot. He's eating sausage. I LOVE sausage! He'll give me a bite. He will. I know it. I'll sit here and sit here and he'll give me a bite. Oh look, here it comes. He's got a piece of sausage in his fingers. He's gonna toss it. He's gonna toss it so I can get it. I'm gonna get it! I'm gonna get that sausage! Out of my way, people, that sausage is mine!

The sausage flies through the air. I start running. I see it. It's up there. I'm gonna get it. I open my mouth.

Hey! A tiny squirrel grabs the sausage. And runs up the tree. That's my snack. Mine! Give that back to me, tiny squirrel!

JASMINE: Those chipmunks are so cute.

ELLIOT: Wedgie hates them.

JASMINE: Why don't you like the chipmunks, Wedgie? They're so sweet.

ELLIOT: Dad, can we go fishing?

DAD: Sure thing.

JASMINE: Yay!

JACKSON: Fishing? I wanna go fishing!

I look up the tree. I see you, Tiny Squirrel. I see you and you have my snack. I'm so mad at you, Tiny Squirrel.

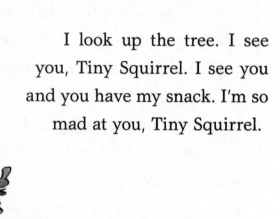

That's my snack and you took it. I feel sad. Tiny Squirrel took my snack.

Elliot's calling me. But I want to stay here. I want to keep barking at Tiny Squirrel. Elliot grabs my collar and pulls me away. Good-bye, Tiny Squirrel! Where are we going? Elliot's taking off my cape. He's putting something around my middle.

ELLiOT: Stop wiggling, Wedgie. We all have to wear life jackets.

Now he's picking me up and carrying me away from my cape. But my cape's back there. I want my cape. I need my cape. I need to wear it so I can protect my pack from the tiny squirrels. If I don't have my cape, the tiny squirrels will steal all our stuff!

Please oh please oh please can I have my cape?

Hey! Furry Potato's outside. Don't worry,

Furry Potato. I'll be back. And then I'll get my cape and I'll be Super Wedgie again.

I'll protect you from the tiny squirrels, Furry Potato!

CHAPTER **13**

GIZMO

WHAT DO I SPY WITH MY LITTLE EVIL EYE?

Thorgi's cape!

Well, well, well. What a lovely way to start the day. There it is, lying on that rock, all by itself, whilst the canine is being carried away. Good-bye, you four-legged fool!

I take a deep breath of morning air and stretch my little legs. This is my first public appearance in this part of the world, so I take my time and stroll around the toilet paper tube, waving up at the trees. The birds gaze down upon me. I bow a few times. I do not hear applause but then remember that birds cannot clap. This is probably the most exciting moment in their feathered lives.

Perhaps I should make a speech. I open my mouth to say something important when an object falls from the tree and bonks me on the head. Egads! It's a greasy piece of breakfast meat. I shake my fist. "How dare you? I do not eat meat!"

Sounds erupt in the tree closest to me. The branches begin to shake. Are we having an earthquake? But then I notice the eyes, dozens of them, looking out from between the tree's branches. I know these creatures. They are chipmunks, rodents of the family Sciuridae. They have striped tails and are known to be mischief makers. They would be perfect in my Evil Horde!

"Greetings," I say. "I am Gizmo the Evil Genius, your future king. Will you come forth and take my Evil Pledge?"

In case you would also like to become a member of my Evil Horde, dear reader, here is a copy of the Evil Oath. Simply raise your right hand and repeat these words:

I, (state your full name), do solemnly swear to serve and obey King Gizmo, the Evil Genius, in all his Evil Doings, including:
Marching and Stomping,
Pillaging and Plundering,
and Marshmallow Munching,
for the glory of the cavy uprising and domination of the world.
Muh-ha-ha!

One of the chipmunks scurries down the tree trunk. I am envious of its ability to travel upside down. I could use that skill in my future Evil Doings. He will be the first chipmunk to take the Evil Oath. I clear my throat and raise my right paw.

"Repeat after me," I say. "I, state your full name . . ."

But the critter runs past me.

What's this? It climbs the rock and begins to sniff the cape.

Another chipmunk races down the tree and also heads toward the cape. Then the two chipmunks grab the edge of the cape in their paws and begin to carry it toward me.

How nice of them. They are already acting as my loyal servants. I snicker with glee and reach out my paws.

Victory is almost mine!

CHAPTER **14**

WEDGIE

WHAT'S THIS THING AROUND MY TUMMY?
It's tight. I don't love this thing. How come I
don't get to wear my cape?

Dad lifts me and puts me into a boat. It's
tippy. I walk to this side. It tips. I walk to
that side. It tips. This is fun. Back and forth,
back and forth. Tip this way, tip that way. I
wish I had my cape. Can I have my cape?

DAD: Okay, you two, do the life jackets fit?

ELLIOT: Mine seems fine.

JASMINE: Mine too.

DAD: Mom and I will be right here on the beach with Jackson. Don't go out too far. Stay close where we can see you.

JACKSON: I wanna go.

MOM: Sweetie, you're too little to go without a grown-up.

JACKSON: But Wedgie's little and he's going.

DAD: You're too young to fish with those sharp hooks. We'll teach you when you get older.

JACKSON: Why am I always too little?

Jackson sounds sad. Why does Jackson sound sad? Does he want to pet me? You can pet me, Jackson. I'll come back so you can pet me.

But Elliot and Jasmine get into the boat. What are we doing? Are we going somewhere? Where are we going? I wag my rump. Elliot puts some sticks into the water and now we're moving. We're floating. I LOVE floating! I stand on my hind legs and look at the water. Hey, there's a dog in the water! Hi, dog! I want to sniff that dog!

JASMINE: Ha-ha! Wedgie's barking at his reflection. Silly boy. That's you.

ELLIOT: It's cool that Mom and Dad are letting us row around by ourselves.

JASMINE: Yeah. I hope we catch a fish.

ELLIOT: I feel a little bad that Jackson can't come with us. Is he crying?

JASMINE: He'll be okay. I didn't get to go fishing when I was his age. He just has to wait to grow up, like I did.

What's that thing? Jasmine's holding something and it's wiggling. I smell it. It's a worm. Worms smell like dirt. I grab it out of Jasmine's hand. I gobble it. Blech! I don't love worms.

Jasmine gets another worm. I don't want to eat that worm. She puts it onto something, then she sticks it into the water. I look into the water. Why's that worm in the water? And why's that dog still in the water? I want to get into the water and meet that dog.

I start to climb but Jasmine grabs me. She

says an important word. The word is *Nowedgie*. I stop climbing. *Nowedgie* is my name when I'm doing something bad. *Nowedgie* means to stop doing whatever I'm doing. So I stop climbing. I walk to the other side of the boat and look into the water. Hey, there's another dog over here!

What's that sound? It's coming from far away. It sounds like Furry Potato. He's squeaking. Is something wrong? I run back to the other side of the boat. I see Mom. I see Dad. I see Jackson. They're all on the beach. But I don't see Furry Potato. He squeaks again. There he is. Way over there by the big tree.

Then I see the tiny squirrels. They're taking my cape! Hey! That's my cape! Mine!

JASMINE: Wedgie, stop doing that; you're gonna tip the boat.
ELLIOT: Wedgie! No, Wedgie!

I'm in the water. It's cold. Water goes up my nose. I sneeze. I'm paddling my legs. There's a bug in the water. Hello, bug! There's a turtle in the water. Hello, turtle! I'm paddling. I'm paddling because I'm gonna get those tiny squirrels. Here I come, tiny squirrels. I'm gonna get you!

I climb out of the water. I'm wet all over. I don't like this feeling so I shake and shake and shake. That's better. Jasmine's calling my name, but I need to get my cape away from those tiny squirrels. I run as fast as I can. Bad tiny squirrels. Bad! Give me my cape, tiny squirrels!

The tiny squirrels run up the tree. Way up there. And now my cape's way up there too. I can't jump that high. I whimper. I'm so sad. Please come down, cape.

DAD: What's going on? Why are you back so soon?

ELLIOT: Wedgie jumped out of the boat.

JASMINE: He scared all the fish away.

DAD: Come on, let's go dry off that silly dog.

ELLIOT: No one in the entire campground will be able to catch a fish now, thanks to Wedgie!

CHAPTER 15

Gizmo

ATTENTION! THIS IS AN IMPORTANT MESSAGE from Gizmo the Evil Genius. We have a situation.

I recently discovered that the chipmunks who live at the Chipmunk Lake Campground do not want to join my Evil Horde. Why? Because they have their own Evil Horde! And they have taken Thorgi's cape to their Evil Lair, which is hidden amongst the branches of a massive pine tree.

The chipmunks want to create their own Evil Empire. Can you imagine? Chipmunks ruling the world? How silly. I knock on the toilet paper tube. "Do you see what is happening here?" I ask Butterball. "The local chipmunks have mutinied against me." She says nothing. I peek into the tube. She is snoring. The fate of the world is at stake and she is asleep! How rude!

I fold my arms and furrow my brow. I want that cape but how might I get it? Cavies are excellent jumpers, but we do not have suction-cup toes like tree frogs and are not built for climbing. Gravity is our enemy because our lower halves are heavier than our upper halves. Reminder to self: when we return home, order antigravity boots, size xxxxxxxsmall.

How else might I get up that tree? Alas, I do not have my Drone of Destiny, nor do I have access to the internet to order another one. But why should I do the work myself?

I place my paws around my mouth. "Listen up, creatures of the forest. Your future king needs one of you to climb a tree! Send out a raccoon or a pair of rats!" I await a reply. "A monkey would do nicely!" Where is everyone? "If a sloth is all you have, I will wait!"

I imagine my new Evil Horde. The mice will gather seeds for me. The beavers will

build my Evil Lair. The ravens will carry my messages near and far.

I tap my foot. "Hello?" No one comes to help me. What a very rude forest!

Then I am struck by a Genius Idea. I shall make a rope ladder. I could weave the rope from grasses as my ancestors once did. Then I could toss it around a branch and climb the rungs straight to the cape. Brilliant! But this will require a lot of walking around, picking grass blades, and carrying them back to camp. I might break a sweat! And the weaving would tire my paws. I might even break a nail. I stick my head into the tube.

"Ball of Butter," I say, "I have a project for you. I will forgive you for invading my home and stealing my food if you weave me a rope ladder." I wait for her response. "As your future king, I order you to do this." She keeps snoring.

I am outraged! Butterball is no help whatsoever. She chooses to nap rather than

change history. I stomp my foot. I will be rid
of her once and for all. I roll the toilet paper
tube until I find a little hill and then I give
it a push.

"Good riddance!" I cry as the tube tum-
bles out of sight. I smile with satisfaction. No
longer will I have to deal with that invader
who wants to eat my SSS. Problem solved!
Now to deal with those chipmunks.

MOM: Time for lunch.

Lunch? My tummy growls. Lunch is my favorite meal of the day. Breakfast, supper, second breakfast, and late-night snack are my second-favorite meals. An Evil Genius cannot work on an empty stomach. Before I begin to weave my rope ladder, I must have something to eat. I waddle back into the tent and settle into my Eco Habitat just as Elliot shows up with an offering of cheddar cheese chunk, apple slice, and carrot stick. Once my belly is full, I curl up for my post-lunch nap.

Just you wait, Evil Chipmunks. When Gizmo the Evil Genius awakens, the Evil Games will begin!

CHAPTER **16**

WEDGIE

JASMINE: Has anyone seen Wedgie's cape? I can't find it.

CHAPTER **17**

GIZMO

WHEN I WAKE FROM MY NAP I FIND THAT evening has fallen. Uh-oh. I slept longer than I had planned. I do hope Thorgi is still without his cape. Just as I am about to go look, Elliot reaches into my Eco Habitat and carries me outside. I peer over his fingers as we walk across the campsite. Yes! The cape is still in the tree! I cast an Evil Smile at the canine. Without his cape, he is a weak fool who cannot stop me. But what if one of the humans sees it and returns it to him? I cannot allow that to happen! I must have it!

The humans are gathered around a campfire. Elliot sits on a log and sets me on his lap. I find it quite relaxing to watch the flames flicker. I feast on a lovely meal of hot-dog bun, carrot stick, and potato chip. My belly is content, my face is warm.

But there is Evil Work to be done!

Important announcement, dear reader. I have decided not to wander the woods searching for grass blades with which to weave a rope ladder. Instead I shall make the ladder out of nearby equipment. That is when I spy the laces on Elliot's shoes. And on Jasmine's shoes. And on Jackson's shoes. If I can tie them together, it will be a perfect ladder! I slide down Elliot's leg and sit on his shoe. Then, using my perfectly sharp teeth, I begin to chew the knot. I wish the ball of butter was here to help me. We rodents are excellent chewers.

MOM: Elliot, what's Gizmo doing?

ABUELA: He's going to make something. He's an evil genius.

ELLIOT: He's not making anything, Abuela. He just likes to chew.

MOM: He's ruining your new shoes. Give him something else to chew.

What's this? Elliot hands me a piece of dried banana. It tastes delicious. I look over at the cape and the canine. The cape appears to be staying in one place, high up on a branch, and the canine appears to be making no progress in getting it. And the Evil Chipmunks have all gone to bed. Since nothing is happening, I suppose I could take a quick snack break.

Elliot stretches out on a blanket and I stretch next to him. As I nibble the dried banana, we gaze up at the night sky. The stars are much brighter out here in the wilderness.

MOM: Wedgie, stop whimpering. The chipmunks are gone.

DAD: Elliot, do you remember the name of that constellation?

ELLIOT: It's called Ursa Major, the greater she-bear.

JASMINE: Is there a dog constellation?

ELLIOT: Yes, but you can't see it during summer. It's called Canis Major, the greater dog. And there's a star called the dog star.

JASMINE: You hear that, Wedgie? There's a star named after you. Doesn't that make you feel better?

Unbelievable. Who would name a star after a canine? And how many times must I correct these humans? The constellation known as Canis Major is misnamed and looks nothing like a dog. Its true name is Cavia Major—the greater cavy. The stars form the shape of a warrior cavy, not a lowly canine. Don't you agree, dear reader?

When I am King of the World, I shall pass a law that Canis Major be officially changed to Cavia Major. And the dog star will be renamed the Gizmo star. Perhaps all constellations should be changed. Why should a bear and a horse get a place in the sky? Only cavies deserve to roam the heavens!

As I am making these plans, Elliot hands me another dried banana. How lovely. If he continues to be my loyal servant, I might name one of the stars after him. My little ears prickle. What's that I hear? The sound of a bag opening? The scent of marshmallow drifts up my nostrils. The humans are about to cook my favorite food over the fire. I quiver. How I want one!

But they will not share. I narrow my eyes. If Elliot wants a star named after him, then he must learn to share his marshmallows. I take another bite of banana. One day I will own all the marshmallow factories and no one, I repeat, no one will keep them from me ever again! I waddle to his shoe and begin chewing. This lace will be mine!

JASMINE: Why won't Wedgie stop whining?

ABUELA: He wants his cape.

JASMINE: But I looked everywhere and I couldn't find it.

JACKSON: I'll find it!

JASMINE: Don't be silly, Jackson. If I couldn't find it then you won't be able to find it.

I pull the shoelace free. But where is the youngest human going? I stand on my hind legs. He's walking over to the canine. He's whispering in the canine's ear. Is he going to help him? No, no, no, no! I jump up and down.

"Stop him!" I holler. "I command you! Stop that child!"

CHAPTER 18

Wedgie

JACKSON HAS MY CAPE. I *LOVE* JACKSON and I LOVE my cape! He ties it around my neck. Look at me. I'm Super Wedgie again! Jackson hugs me. I lick his face. I look into his eyes. He sits in the dirt and hugs me some more. He knows I was sad about my cape. He whispers in my ear.

JACKSON: I'm *not* too little.

Jackson's sad because the tiny squirrels took my cape. Don't worry, Jackson. I'll chase those tiny squirrels away. You can count on me because I'm Super Wedgie again. Day or night, night or day, I'll get rid of those tiny squirrels, come what may!

Furry Potato is squeaking. Don't worry, Furry Potato. I'm Super Wedgie again.

CHAPTER 19

Gizmo

ONCE AGAIN, THE SCREECHING OF BIRDS wakes the entire forest. Must they have choir practice at six a.m.? How very rude. I have made a list of rude creatures and here it is for your information:

GIZMO'S LIST OF THE ALL-TIME RUDEST CREATURES
1. Birds who sing in the morning.
2. Chipmunks who bonk you on the head with bits of cooked meat.
3. Hamsters who sneak into your Eco Habitat and eat all your food.
4. All canines . . . because of everything they do!

I yawn and stretch my little legs. It is the start of another Evil Day and, as usual, I have much to accomplish. In case you have forgotten, let me remind you. Yesterday I completed goal #1, which was to get rid of the stowaway and thief known as Butterball. She is gone. I am amazing.

As I nibble on a blueberry, I think about the stowaway. Should I feel bad that I pushed her into the wilderness? No, I should not! She had plenty of food stored in her cheeks. And the toilet paper tube will serve as a bed and shelter. She can now join her fellow hamsters in the wild and live totally free. I will expect to receive a thank-you card from her very soon.

DAD: Is everyone ready to hike to the top of Chipmunk Waterfall?

JACKSON: Hike!

MOM: Jackson, we're hiking two miles. You're too little to go that far. You stay here with Abuela and Wedgie.

DAD: We'll do a fun hike with you when we get back!

MOM: Yes, a *little* hike.

JACKSON: (sigh)

ELLIOT: Sorry, Wedgie, you can't come with us either. They don't allow dogs on the trails.

As I finish a second blueberry, Elliot reaches into my Eco Habitat. Oh no! Not another field trip! Will these humans ever check my appointment calendar? I do not have time for this! I must focus on goal #2—to get Thorgi's cape! And then I have a campground to conquer!

ELLIOT: Come on, Gizmo, stop squirming. We're gonna have fun.

Fun? Evil Geniuses do not have fun. We mastermind Evil Plans! But I do not want to be unprepared, so I grab my Barbie Binoculars. Elliot picks me up and carries me outside. Then he sets me onto his shoulder and hands me a peanut.

We leave the tent. The Evil Chipmunks are sitting in their Evil Tree. I shake my fist at them. "I do not know where my servant is taking me, but when I return I will summon all the forest critters into my Evil Horde and you will all be vanquished!"

Then I glance down at the canine, who is running around the tree. "As for you, Thorgi, when I return, my new Evil Horde will steal your cape!"

But first, I must eat this lovely peanut.

The humans begin to follow a path through the woods. The parents take the lead, with Jasmine in the middle and Elliot and I in the rear. Sitting on Elliot's shoulder provides me an excellent view of the world I will one day rule.

MOM: Isn't it nice that Elliot and Jasmine are getting along so well?

DAD: Yeah. Being outside is good for them.

JASMINE: Wow, look at that huge mushroom.

ELLIOT: That's so cool! Look at that bird nest.

To be King of the World means the *entire*

world, and that includes neighborhoods like the one back home, villages, cities, islands, and forests. It even includes the oceans. I should add field trips to my calendar so that I can begin to see all the places I will rule and meet the strange creatures who live there.

Strange creatures like the one that is currently hovering in front of me. It is bright blue, with long, lacy wings. I do believe it is called a dragonfly. One of its friends flies next to it; this one is bright red. They stare at me.

I have long considered insects to be inferior, since they have brains the size of a grain of sand. But insects *are* interesting, for they do not think as individuals. They have a hive mind, meaning they work as a group. Many have a queen. Oh, how perfect! If they will follow a queen then surely they will follow a king. I shall invite these insects to join my Evil Horde.

"Greetings," I say. "My name is—"

The blue dragonfly lands on my head. For a moment, I am shocked. I look over at Elliot. Hello? Do you not see this? There is a dragonfly sitting on my head!

ELLIOT: Did you guys see that blue jay?

JASMINE: So pretty!

ELLIOT: There's another one.

Why is my servant looking at those birds? There is a bug on my head! I swat at the creature. Be gone! But it does not move. To make matters worse, the red one lands on my head. My head is not a public bench.

How dare they treat their future king in this manner?

ELLIOT: Gizmo, stop moving around. You're gonna fall off.

I swat again. And again. Alas, my little arms cannot reach them. Elliot, my loyal servant, why do you not help me? Get off—

Whoops. I teeter. I totter. Now I am falling! Plummeting to a ghastly death. Oh, dear reader, look away. Cover your eyes, for this will most certainly be the most gruesome demise in history.

Plunk!

I am happy to report that I land in a soft pile of leaves. But the fall causes me to lose my balance and I roll onto my side, then keep rolling, down an embankment. The world is a blurry place. I roll and roll.

Will I ever stop rolling? Help!

CHAPTER **20**

WEDGIE

I'M SITTING BY THE LAKE. JACKSON'S SITTING with me. Abuela's here too. I stick my paw into the water. It's cold. I stick my other paw into the water. It's still cold. I stick my nose into the water. Wow, that's really cold. I sneeze.

ABUELA: Jackson, why so sad?

JACKSON: Elliot and Jasmine won't play with me. They think I can't do anything!

ABUELA: Look at me, young man. How did you know how to catch that fish?

JACKSON: I saw one eat a little water bug.

ABUELA: How did you know how to climb that tree?

JACKSON: I watched a little chipmunk.

ABUELA: You see. You're smarter than the rest because you look at the small things. Let's go for a walk and see what we can find.

Abuela's walking. Jackson's walking. Where are we going? I follow them. Abuela gets my leash. She wants me to take her for a walk. I LOVE going for a walk! We're gonna piddle on things. But then Abuela ties my leash to a tree. Hey, I don't like being tied to a tree.

ABUELA: What a fuss you're making, Wedgie. You only have to stay here for a short while.

Where are you going? I wanna go too. I try to follow but I'm tied to a tree. I try to get untied. I wind this way. I get stuck so I wind that way. I get stuck again. Am I a Bad Dog? Why are you going and why am I staying?

Jackson and Abuela are gone. I'm all

alone. I whimper. I don't like being all alone. When will my family come back? Hello? Hello? Where are you, family?

NO DOGS ON THE TRAILS

I hear a squeak. Then another. Oh no!
Here come the tiny squirrels. They're run-
ning down the tree. They're running all over
my new yard. One of them grabs a sock. It's
Jackson's sock. Let go of that sock! Super
Wedgie will get the sock. I pull real hard. I
pull harder. I use my superpower of pulling.
I pull right out of my collar. I'm free! Super
Wedgie to the rescue!

I chase them into the tent. Then out of
the tent.

I chase them around the food and over
the food.

I chase them into the boat and out of the
boat.

I'm such a good dog because I'm chasing
the tiny squirrels!

Day or night, night or day, Super Wedgie
will get that sock, come what may!

CHAPTER 21

GIZMO

DEAR READER, DO NOT DESPAIR. EVEN THOUGH I rolled straight down a mountain, I am not injured, thanks to my amazing gymnastic skills and my extra padding. My glasses are in perfect working order. However, I seem to have lost my Barbie Binoculars during the tumble. As I pick twigs from my fur, I sit and think about my situation.

Surely I cannot be expected to hike back

up that hill. Evil Geniuses do not hike! We are carried by our loyal servants or by Drones of Destiny. Perhaps I should simply sit still, waiting for rescue. Surely Elliot has already sent out a search party. I listen for my name being called. And for sirens blasting as the search and rescue troops arrive. But I only hear the trickle of a nearby stream.

Water! All that tumbling has made me thirsty.

I wipe dirt from my glasses, then I follow the sound. Why is the forest so crowded with plants? There are sticks and leaves and rocks everywhere. Someone should pick up this mess! When I am King of the World I shall employ a herd of goats to eat every forest until it is sparkling clean.

I climb over a broken branch. My paws are getting dirty. I will need to make a visit to the Pretty Pets Salon when I get home, for a relaxing bubble bath. As I step around a toadstool, a beetle crawls into my path.

"Out of my way!" I command. "Your future king is thirsty!" Then I stare into its black eyes. "This is your lucky day. Raise your right hand . . . or paw . . . or whatever that is, and repeat after me. I . . . insert your name here . . ."

The beetle walks away.

How rude!

I groan. How long have I been in this forsaken wilderness? Five minutes? Alas, I am done for. I must summon courage, like the wild cavies who roam the Andes mountains. They do not have a servant, nor an Eco Habitat with an air-conditioned sleeping chamber. I will use my Evil Brain to survive. I will find the trail, then follow it back to the human campsite, where the Elderly One will feed me a cheesy puff and the birds will sing a joyous song to celebrate my return.

Why can I not find the stream? Are there no signs in this primeval forest? As soon as I get home, I shall write a nasty review of this place.

"The forest surrounding the Chipmunk Lake Campground has too many plants and not enough paved roads. And not a single spa to be found!"

Zero stars from Gizmo the Evil Genius

Oh, I feel so weary. My little legs are not used to this sort of stress. I stop a moment to catch my breath. This is the fault of those pesky dragonflies. They must be in cahoots with the Evil Chipmunks. Won't they be surprised when I return to the campsite in perfect health? When I am King of the World I shall feed all dragonflies to my Evil Lizard Army!

Finally I reach the stream. At home, Elliot always fills my water bottle with glacier water from Iceland. He does this for he knows that only special water should pass my lips.

But here I am, about to drink from a stream. Oh, the humiliation! I lean over until my mouth comes in contact with the crisp, cool water. I drink. To my surprise, this is perhaps the best water I have ever tasted. I lean closer to take another drink and . . .

Splash!

Do not fear, for we cavies are excellent swimmers. I pop to the surface, then reach for a branch, pulling myself onto the shore. I am safe, but the freezing temperature has soaked all the way through my fur. I sit on a rock and wrap my arms around my middle. So very, very cold. I shiver from the tips of my paws to the top of my Genius Head. How shall I survive if I am too frozen to walk?

My tummy growls. Where is a cheesy snack when I need it? I wish I had hamster cheeks filled with food. Oh, will someone not save me? "Help!"

Someone answers me with a squeak. I push aside a leaf and what do I see? Is it a spa? Is it a French restaurant? No.

What I see is a toilet paper tube!

CHAPTER 22

WEDGIE

DAD: Abuela, what happened? The campsite is a disaster.

ABUELA: Looks like the dog went chipmunk chasing.

MOM: Bad dog, Wedgie.

I'm a Bad Dog? Why am I a Bad Dog? Those tiny squirrels are bad. See them up there in our tree? They broke our new house and our new boat. And they took more socks.

I run around the tree. I see you, tiny squirrels. I see you way up there. I'm Super Wedgie and I'm gonna get those socks!

ELLIOT: Mom, Dad, we don't have time to worry about the campsite. Gizmo's in the woods somewhere. He's going to get eaten if we don't find him.

How can I get the socks? Can I use my powers of staring? I will try. I sit under the tree and stare. And stare and stare and stare. Something bonks me on the head. It's a pinecone. Hey, those tiny squirrels bonked me with a pinecone! Oh, I do not love tiny squirrels!

DAD: It's too dark to go back into the woods. We'll have to wait until first light to continue our search.

ELLIOT: But what if something eats Gizmo?

ABUELA: He does look tasty.

ELLIOT: This is all my fault. I didn't catch him when he fell!

JASMINE: Elliot, please don't cry. We'll find Gizmo.

ELLIOT: What if we don't?

JACKSON: Look what I found.

ELLIOT: I don't want to play right now, Jackson. I'm too sad.

Elliot's sad. He sits on a log. I sit next to him and put my head in his lap. Don't be sad, Elliot. I'll get our socks back. I promise. And I'll chase those tiny squirrels out of our new tree and out of our new yard.

Hey, Furry Potato's house is empty. Where's Furry Potato?

CHAPTER 23

GIZMO

IMAGINE MY SURPRISE WHEN BUTTERBALL
climbs out of the toilet paper tube. She looks
different. Her face is smaller. And then I
notice a pile of seeds and treats at her feet.
She squeaks at me, then holds out a sunflower seed.

Normally I would not eat a sunflower
seed that has traveled in someone's cheek
pouch. How disgusting! But having missed
lunch, my post-lunch snack, my presupper

snack, and supper itself, I am near starvation. I take the seed and devour it! Oh, the glory of food! I eat another, and another, and together we enjoy a meal of soggy seeds.

When my tummy is full, I sit back and observe Butterball for a moment. Perhaps I misjudged this hamster. I thought she was a stowaway, but now I see the truth. She left Bob's Pet Store to serve me. Of course! She is my new loyal servant.

I nod my head at her. How lucky she is to be serving me. She will probably send me a second thank-you letter. I pick a bit of sunflower husk from my teeth. Do you see how brilliant I am, dear reader? If I had not pushed the ball of butter into the forest, she would not be here to supply me with food. What an Evil Genius I am!

Evening has arrived. There is no sign of Elliot or the search party. As the sky darkens and as the first stars appear, a terrible thought hits me. Will I be forced to sleep out here tonight? Must I make a nest from leaves and moss like a wild creature? Butterball has her toilet paper tube, but where will I lay my Evil Head? On the *ground*?

The sounds of the night are unsettling. From a branch a pair of glowing eyes appears, as round as coins. A hooting sound fills the air, followed by the flapping of wings as the eyes take flight. "Watch out!" I holler.

Butterball squeezes into her tube. I try to follow, but alas, I am too round. As fast as my little legs can carry me, I scramble into a hole. Just in time! The owl flies away.

But as I take a deep breath, something pinches my rump. I scurry out of the hole and look back. A reptilian face glares at me. Then it darts its forked tongue. The creature is unwilling to share the hole. How rude!

In the distance, the owl hoots again. I am standing in the open, with nothing to protect me. Surely the owl will not be able to resist me. The flapping sound gets closer. I must use my Evil Brain. Think, Gizmo! How can I save myself? I have so much to accomplish. An entire world to conquer. This cannot be my doom!

Butterball squeaks at me. She sticks her little arm out of the tube and points to a large leaf that is lying on the ground. The answer comes to me like a bolt of lightning. Camou-flage. I must blend in with my surroundings.

And so I lie down on the leaf, cling to one edge, and begin to roll myself up. I roll until I am snug in the leaf like a pea in a pod. The sound of flapping rushes past me. I have tricked the owl. Oh, clever me!

This will be a long night and I hope that when we meet again, dear reader, I will have survived.

CHAPTER 24

WEDGIE

I'M SITTING IN FRONT OF THE TENT. I'M guarding Jackson's socks. If any of those tiny squirrels tries to get into this tent and take Jackson's socks, I'll growl and I'll bark and I'll scare them away. And I won't let them in. Those are Jackson's socks and I'm the only one who gets to chew them and bury them. So stay away, you tiny squirrels! Stay away from me, and stay away from this tent, and stay away from Jackson's socks!

Grrrrrrr.

ELLIOT: Dad, the sun's up. We gotta go look
for Gizmo. Come on!

DAD: This early? (yawn)

ELLIOT: Dad!

DAD: Yeah, okay, okay. I'm awake. Let's go
find him.

JASMINE: I'm awake too. I'm gonna help.

MOM: Abuela, please watch Wedgie while
we're gone. I don't want to have to
clean up another mess.

ABUELA: What do I look like? A dog sitter? Go
ask Jackson.

MOM: He's still asleep.

Mom and Dad and Jasmine and Elliot are
walking into the woods. They're leaving me
here because they want me to keep the tiny
squirrels out of our yard. I'm ready. I piddled. I ate my kibble. I piddled some more.

And now I'm here, in front of the tent. Don't come near this tent, tiny squirrels. These socks are mine!

Grrrrrrr.

My eyes feel kinda heavy. I close them. Just for a little while.

Zzzzzzzz.

My eyes fly open. Hey! There's a tiny squirrel in the tent. He's digging through Jackson's backpack. Now he's got a sock. He's trying to steal it. I grab one end of the sock and pull. The tiny squirrel holds the other end. He pulls. I pull. He's a strong tiny squirrel. But Super Wedgie's stronger and I yank the sock away. It's mine! The tiny squirrel looks at me. Then he runs back up the tree. He's got something in his paw. It smells real good. Whatcha got in your paw, tiny squirrel? It's a piece of sausage. He throws it into the air. I open my mouth. The sock falls to the ground but I don't care. I catch the sausage. I LOVE sausage!

But now the tiny squirrel has the sock and he takes it right up the tree.

ABUELA: Good morning, Jackson.
JACKSON: Wedgie jumped on me and woke me up. Silly Wedgie.

I'm sad about the sock, but I'm happy I got a piece of sausage. Can I have more? Hey, tiny squirrels? Do you have more sausage? I scratch on the tree. Can you hear me, tiny squirrels?

ABUELA: Jackson, do you remember where you found those little binoculars?

JACKSON: Yes.

ABUELA: Then show me.

A tiny squirrel runs down the tree. He goes into the tent. He comes out with a sock. Hey! That's Elliot's sock! I grab the end of the sock. I pull. Tiny squirrel pulls. I pull. He pulls. I yank the sock away. It's mine! The tiny squirrel runs up the tree. He's got something in his paw. It smells real good. It's sausage! I open my mouth. The sock falls to the ground. Yum! I got another sausage!

I scratch on the tree. Can I have more? I scratch and scratch. Hello? It's me, Super Wedgie, waiting for more sausage. Come back, tiny squirrels. Please come back.

Oh wait, I know what to do. This is like when I play fetch with Dad. If I get the ball, he gives me a treat. I run back into the tent. I dig through Jackson's backpack. Where are all the socks? I sniff around. Socks, where are you? I dig through Jasmine's backpack and find a sock. I run to the tree and drop the sock. Please oh please oh—

I got another sausage!

ABUELA: Wedgie, you stay here. We're going to look for the cavy.

JACKSON: Aren't you gonna tie Wedgie to the tree?

ABUELA: There's no need. The chipmunks are training him.

Here's a sock, tiny squirrels. Give me a sausage. Here's another sock. Give me another sausage. Sock. Sausage. Sock. Sausage.

I LOVE this game!

CHAPTER 25

GIZMO

BIRDSONG WAKES ME ONCE AGAIN. I SLOWLY open my eyes. My entire body feels stiff, as if I had slept on the cold, hard ground.

And then I remember—I *did* sleep on the cold, hard ground. How unpleasant.

I crawl out from my leaf blanket. Then I put my hands on my hips and stand tall and proud. Gizmo the Evil Genius survived a terrifying night in the wilderness. Well done indeed!

When I get back home, I shall write a survival manual with tips on how to survive if lost in the woods.

GIZMO'S GUIDE TO SURVIVING IN THE WILDERNESS
1. Take a hamster with you, to carry extra food.
2. Use camouflage to avoid being eaten.
3. Carry bug spray, especially the kind that works on dragonflies.

"I am hungry," I announce. Butterball pops her head out of the toilet paper tube. I sit on a rock, waiting for breakfast to be served.

My breakfast consists of four soggy sunflower seeds. Not a king's meal but alas, it is the last of our supply. I must be a leader and show Butterball how to gather food. I motion for her to follow. How will she ever learn to be a good servant if she spends all day sleeping?

We search and soon we find berries. Most

are beyond our reach but one of the branches is so heavy with berries that it hangs low. I stand on my hind legs and grab one. It is perfectly round and red. How lovely. I do not know if it is poisonous so I allow Butterball to test it. She eats it and when she does not keel over, I eat one. It is tart but scrumptious.

I shall name these Gizmo berries. While Butterball fills her cheeks, I eat two more handfuls. My tummy now feels full, which means we can begin our trek.

I suspect that it might take the full day to return to camp, my steps being much smaller than Elliot's. I craft a sun hat out of twigs and leaves, to shade my handsome face.

"Come along, Butterball," I say. "We must begin our quest to find the campsite." She pats her toilet paper tube and looks at me. Does she wish to take that on our trek? Surely it will slow us down. I clear my throat, about to inform her that she must leave it behind, but she spits out a little berry and offers it to me. For a moment, I feel . . . touched. How loyal she is. How kind. I eat the berry, then I grab the tube and begin rolling it through the underbelly of the forest.

You might think, dear reader, that I have gone soft, but that is not the case. I am not helping the ball of butter because I am being *nice*. I need someone to carry my food.

Still you do not believe me? Let me make

this perfectly clear—an Evil Genius does not do nice things!

After a few minutes of waddling, I realize that we have been following the stream. I stop and ponder. Does this stream empty into the lake at the human campsite? I spy a turtle sitting on a log. He looks at us with curiosity. The Elderly One and I once watched a documentary about giant tortoises who lived for more than one hundred years. Being so long lived, they must know many things.

I introduce myself to the turtle and ask if the stream leads to the lake. I am surprised when the turtle nods. Joy of joys, he speaks my language! But of course, with all that extra time on his hands, he has learned many languages. I wonder if he would like to take my Evil Oath but we have a long way to travel and must make haste.

Whilst Butterball waits beside her toilet paper tube, I look around for something that will serve as a boat, and I find a large piece of bark. I push it into the water and lo and behold, it floats! Butterball climbs onboard and empties her cheek pouches, leaving a nice, tidy pile of red berries. I set the toilet paper tube next to her and she scurries inside. Then I grab a stick, climb onto our raft, and push off. As we begin to drift downstream, I stand at the helm, taking my place as captain of this vessel. Captain Gizmo. That has a nice ring to it.

I shall join the ranks of other great explorers, the ones who climbed mountains, the ones who sailed to the ends of the earth. I do hope there are no pirates in these waters.

MOM and DAD: Gizmo! Gizmo, where are you?

JASMINE: I'll go look by the stream.

ELLIOT: Be careful you don't step on
him! Gizmo!

The stick helps me navigate as I push us away from rocks and logs. The going is dangerous, but of course I am a skilled seaman. I row a bit on the starboard side, then I row on the port side. Then I make up a little song to the tune of "Row, Row, Row Your Boat."

Row, row, row downstream,
Gizmo leads the way.
He's the captain we adore;
Gizmo saves the day.
Row, row, row downstream,

We don't need a map.
Captain Gizmo charts our course;
He's the greatest chap!

The ball of butter is not singing. How rude.

Row, row, row downstream—

My ship begins to rock. What is causing this motion? I stand on my tiptoes to get a better view. The water is churning and twisting. Oh, great Neptune, the stream is widening! We will be dashed upon the rocks!

Panic rises in my little chest. "All hands on deck!" I cry. Butterball squeaks and pokes out her head. I paddle as fast as I can but I am no match for the rushing waters. I fear the end is near! Good-bye, my loyal followers. Good-bye, dear reader. Good-bye, world!

CHAPTER 26

WEDGIE

I'M A HAPPY DOG. SO VERY, VERY HAPPY. I ATE lots and lots of sausage. And now I'm lying on the ground. It feels good to lie on the ground. I see an ant. Hello, ant! I see another ant. Hello, other ant! I see a piece of tiny squirrel poop but I'm not gonna eat it because it's way over there and I'm way over here and it feels so good to lie here on the ground. I look up at the branches. I can see all the tiny squirrels. I start to growl.

Grr . . .

I don't want to growl. I LOVE the tiny squirrels!

ELLIOT: Dad, we can't stop looking. We need to find him!

DAD: It'll just take a minute to refill our water bottles, then we'll go back. It's getting hot and we need to stay hydrated.

JACKSON: I found Gizmo! I found Gizmo!

ELLIOT: You did? Gizmo! I'm so glad you're safe.

JASMINE: How'd you find him?

ABUELA: Jackson is very good at noticing the little things.

JACKSON: Yes, I am. I found this too. Her name is Butterball.

JASMINE: That's the cutest hamster I've ever seen! What's she doing in the woods?

Hey! What's everyone looking at? Do I need to get up? Do I need to go see? Yes, I do! Okay, here I come, people! It smells like Furry Potato. It is! It's Furry Potato. Hello, Furry Potato! It's so nice to see you. I LOVE Furry Potato! But what's that new smell? There's something in Jackson's hand. Can I see? I scratch Jackson's shoe. Show me, Jackson. Show me what's in your hand. Why, it's a tiny Furry Potato. I sniff its face.

I sniff its tummy. I sniff its rump. I like the way it smells. It's a real nice, tiny Furry Potato. Are you going to be a new member of my pack? I sure hope so!

ELLIOT: Jackson, thank you for finding Gizmo.

MOM: We're so proud of you, Jackson. You caught a fish. You found Wedgie's cape. And now you found Gizmo.

DAD: I guess you're not too little after all.

JACKSON: Will you play with me now?

ELLIOT: Of course we will. I'm sorry we've been ignoring you.

JASMINE: Me too. Will you help us go around to the other campsites and see if anyone is missing a hamster?

JACKSON: Yay!

Everybody's doing stuff. But I ate a lot of sausage and now I'm gonna lie down over here. Super Wedgie's gonna take a nap, people.

Super Wedgie's off duty for a little while, so if the tiny squirrels want more socks, just let me know. But right now I'm gonna close my eyes and . . .

ZZZZZZZZ.

DAD: Has anyone seen my socks?

CHAPTER 27

GIZMO

SO THERE YOU HAVE IT, DEAR READER. DID you ever doubt that I could find my way out of the wilderness? My sea shanty caught the attention of the humans, just as I planned, and here I am, back at the campsite. The girl child is overjoyed to see me, for she is covering me with kisses. And Elliot, my loyal servant, has presented me with an extra-special meal of a broccoli stem, a tortilla chip, and a crisp lettuce leaf. What would they do without me?

ELLIOT: No one in the campground lost a hamster.

DAD: I called Bob at the pet store and it turns out that Butterball was staying at the pet hotel. She must have climbed into Gizmo's cage and we accidentally took her with us. Her owner is so happy we found her. We'll drop her off on our way home.

JASMINE: But she's so cute. Can't I keep her?

MOM: She has an owner who loves her. How would you feel if someone kept Wedgie?

JASMINE: I'd feel terrible! You're right, we have to give her back.

DAD: Bob said that she's escaped before. He called her a little evil genius.

What's this I hear? I stop chewing. The ball of butter is an *Evil Genius*?

I narrow my eyes and stare at her. Is it true? Does she make Evil Plans? Is her brain the size of three peas? I chuckle to myself. Of course it is not true. There is only one rodent who is an Evil Genius and that is me!

As I continue to nibble, I ponder Evil Plan #1 and Evil Plan #2. Butterball will soon be returned to her human owner, and so my plan to be rid of her is a success. Am I sad that she will not stay and be my servant? Perhaps. But I know that no matter where she lives, she will continue to be my loyal follower and she will spread the word of my Evilness. And when I finally take over the world, I will send for her so that she may continue to serve me. She is so lucky to have met me.

Evil Plan #2, however, is still unfinished. I peer over the top of my lettuce leaf. Thorgi is lying on the ground like one of the stuffed animals in Jasmine's room. He is a lazy creature who does not deserve such a cape. I am determined to have it! *Operation: Get Thorgi's Cape* is the most important thing on my Evil Mind. From this point on I will think of nothing else!

Except for that scent. That delicious scent!

Toasted marshmallows! A shiver of excitement darts up my spine. The humans are sitting around the campfire, making treats that they call s'mores.

JASMINE: Jackson, will you make me a s'more?

MOM: Oh dear. Maybe he shouldn't. The fire is—

ELLIOT: Mom. I think he can do it.

MOM: You're right. He can do it just fine, all by himself.

JACKSON: Yes, I can!

ELLIOT: Sorry, Gizmo, but chocolate and marshmallows aren't good for you.

Fie on those humans for not sharing! "Give me a marshmallow or you shall feel my wrath!" I holler.

But what's this? Butterball is waddling up to me. Her face is looking extra stuffed. She blinks at me. Does she want to thank me for saving her from the dangers of the forest? "You're welcome," I tell her. She opens her mouth and out comes . . . a marshmallow!

Joy of joys, she has managed to steal one without the humans noticing. She is an excellent thief.

We sit side by side, nibbling on the puffy delight. And when we are done, we lie on our backs, staring up at the night sky, our tummies full.

JASMINE: Look, isn't that cute? Gizmo has a friend.

It is important for me to point out that Evil Geniuses do not have friends. We have followers. We have minions. We have Evil Hordes. But still, it is nice to be in the company of another rodent who appreciates my greatness.

And then Butterball hands me a piece of paper.

MY EVIL PLAN by BUTTERBALL THE EVIL GENIUS
1. Make friends with other Evil Geniuses!
2. Create an Evil Genius Secret Society!
3. Start an uprising and take over the world!
Bwa-ha-ha!

So it is true! She is an Evil Genius after all! I should have guessed, for only a genius of the evil variety could find a way to sneak into my Eco Habitat without my knowing. What an interesting turn of events. Perhaps it *is* time for an Evil Genius Secret Society. We could combine our Evil Brain Powers to thwart Thorgi and all the other superheroes who try to stop us. Of course, I would be the president!

ELLIOT: Look, everyone, it's the Big Dipper.

I have made another decision, dear reader. When I become King of the World, I will give Butterball a special place in the heavens.

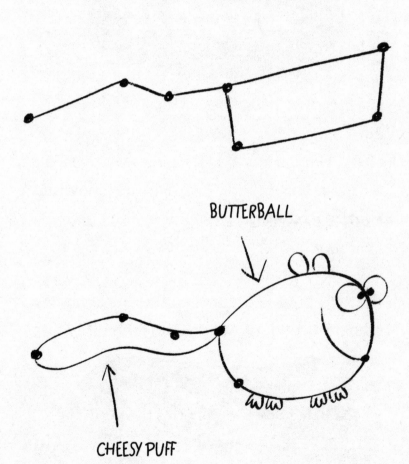

BUTTERBALL

CHEESY PUFF

CHAPTER **28**

WEDGIE

I *LOVE* CAMPING!

Dear Reader,

Do you have what it takes to be a member of Gizmo's Evil Horde? If so, you can take the Evil Oath.

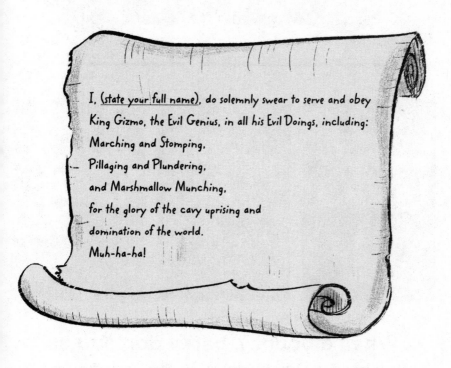

I, (state your full name), do solemnly swear to serve and obey King Gizmo, the Evil Genius, in all his Evil Doings, including:

Marching and Stomping,

Pillaging and Plundering,

and Marshmallow Munching,

for the glory of the cavy uprising and

domination of the world.

Muh-ha-ha!

WEDGIE & GIZMO

When a bouncy, barky dog and an evil genius guinea pig move into the same house, the laughs are nonstop!